JOSEPH MIDTHUN   SAMUEL HITI

BUILDING BLOCKS OF SCIENCE

THE CIRCULATORY SYSTEM

WORLD BOOK

a Scott Fetzer company
Chicago

www.worldbook.com

World Book, Inc.
233 N. Michigan Avenue
Chicago, IL 60601
U.S.A.

For information about other World Book publications,
visit our website at www.worldbook.com
or call 1-800-WORLDBK (967-5325).
For information about sales to schools and libraries,
call 1-800-975-3250 (United States),
or 1-800-837-5365 (Canada).

Library of Congress Cataloging-in-Publication Data

The circulatory system.
    pages cm. -- (Building blocks of science)
  Summary: "A graphic nonfiction volume that
introduces the circulatory system of the human
body"-- Provided by publisher.
  Includes index.
  ISBN 978-0-7166-1842-3
  1. Cardiovascular system--Juvenile literature.
2. Heart--Juvenile literature. 3. Cardiovascular
system--Comic books, strips, etc. 4. Heart--
Comic books, strips, etc. 5. Graphic novels.
I. World Book, Inc.
QP103.C57 2014
612.1--dc23
                          2013024688

Building Blocks of Science
ISBN: 978-0-7166-1840-9 (set, hc.)

Printed in China by Shenzhen Donnelley
Printing Co., Ltd., Guangdong Province
1st printing October 2013

Acknowledgments:
Created by Samuel Hiti and Joseph Midthun
Art by Samuel Hiti
Written by Joseph Midthun
Special thanks to Syril McNally

TABLE OF CONTENTS

There is a glossary on page 30. Terms defined in the glossary are in type **that looks like this** on their first appearance.

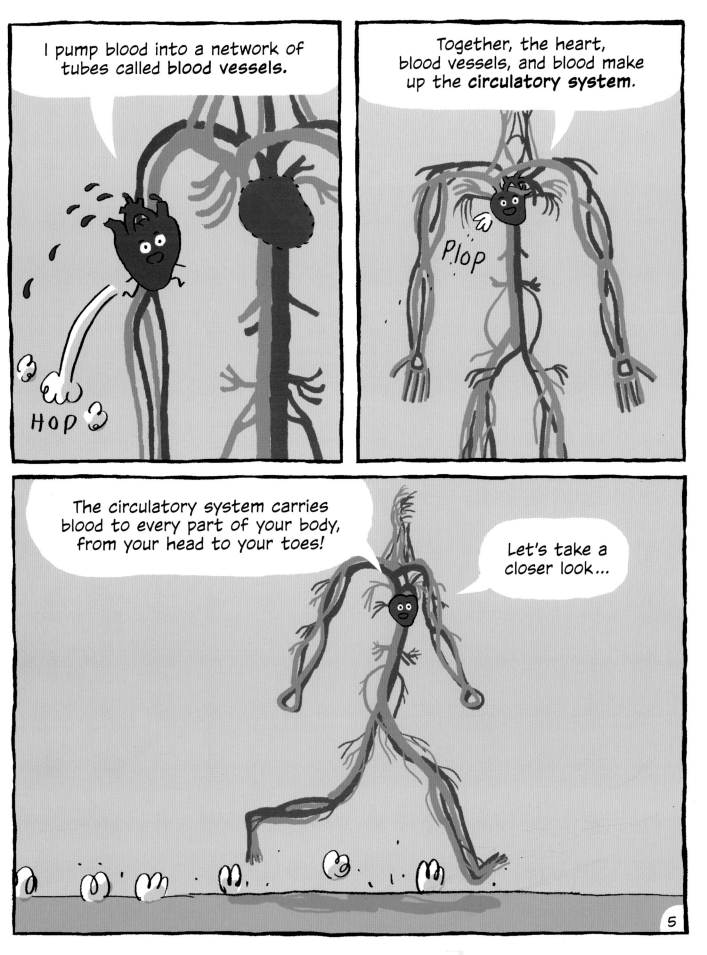

More than half of your blood is made of a watery, pale-yellow liquid called **plasma**.

Blood also contains three different types of blood cells:

RED BLOOD CELLS

PLATELETS

WHITE BLOOD CELLS

Plasma carries these blood cells through blood vessels.

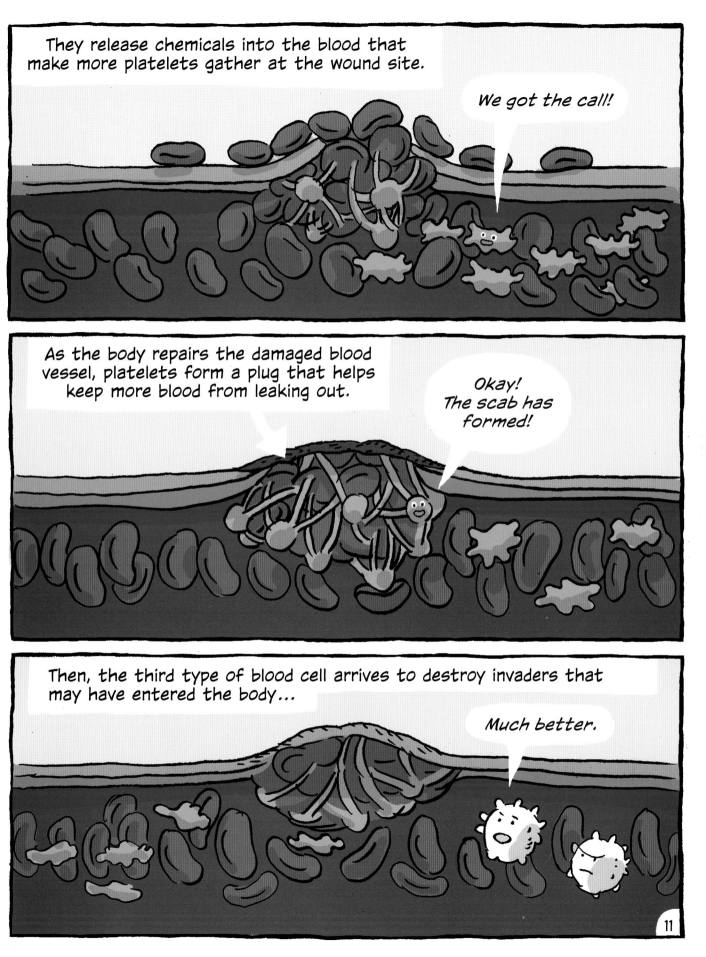

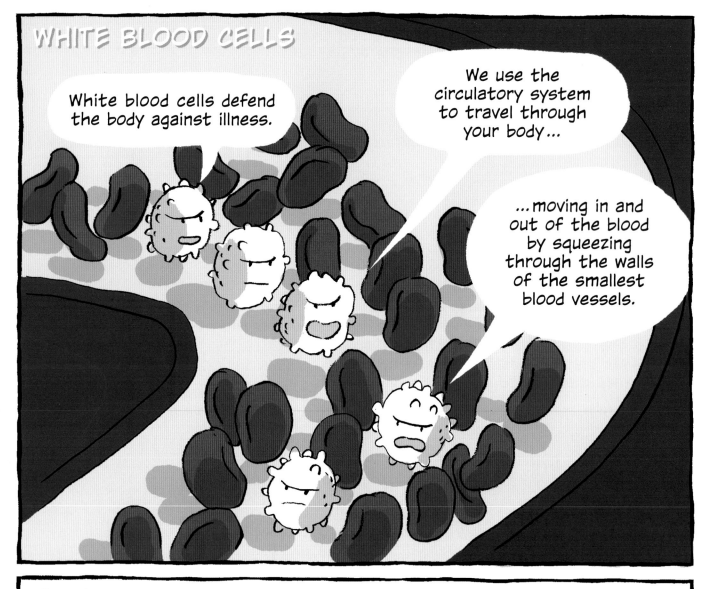

White blood cells work together to attack invaders like **viruses** and **bacteria**.

There are five main types of white blood cell, and each has a particular job.

Some release chemicals to fight disease...

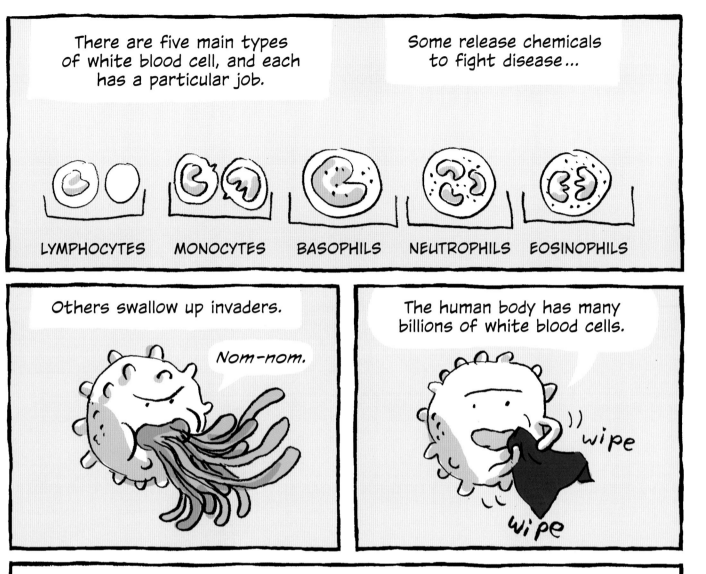

Others swallow up invaders.

The human body has many billions of white blood cells.

When the body is fighting infection, the number of white blood cells increases.

BLOOD VESSELS

All of your blood cells move around your body through blood vessels, including **arteries**, **capillaries**, and **veins**.

Arteries are some of the largest blood vessels.

They carry oxygen-rich blood from your heart to the capillaries.

As the blood flows through the capillaries, oxygen, nutrients, and other substances move from the blood into cells.

14

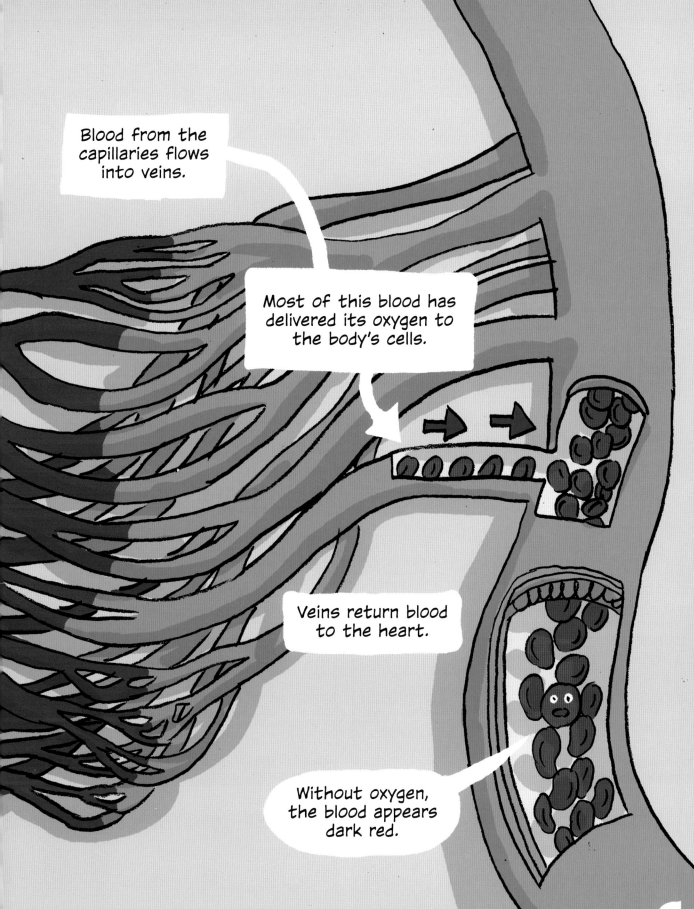

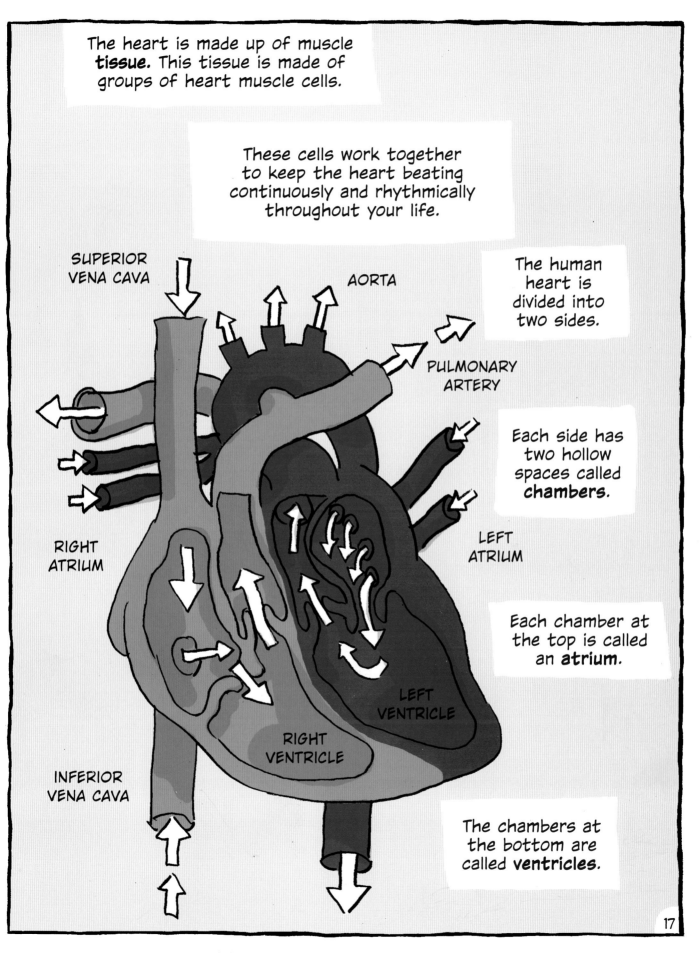

The steady pumping of the heart moves blood through the body.

In fact, the heart is actually **two** pumps working at the same time.

Each pump pushes blood through a separate loop of blood vessels.

The left ventricle pumps oxygen-rich blood through the body.

This blood leaves the heart through the **aorta,** the main artery of the body.

Several major arteries branch off the aorta.

These arteries branch into even smaller blood vessels.

Finally, the arteries empty into tiny capillaries.

Here, oxygen leaves the red blood cells and enters the tissues through capillary walls.

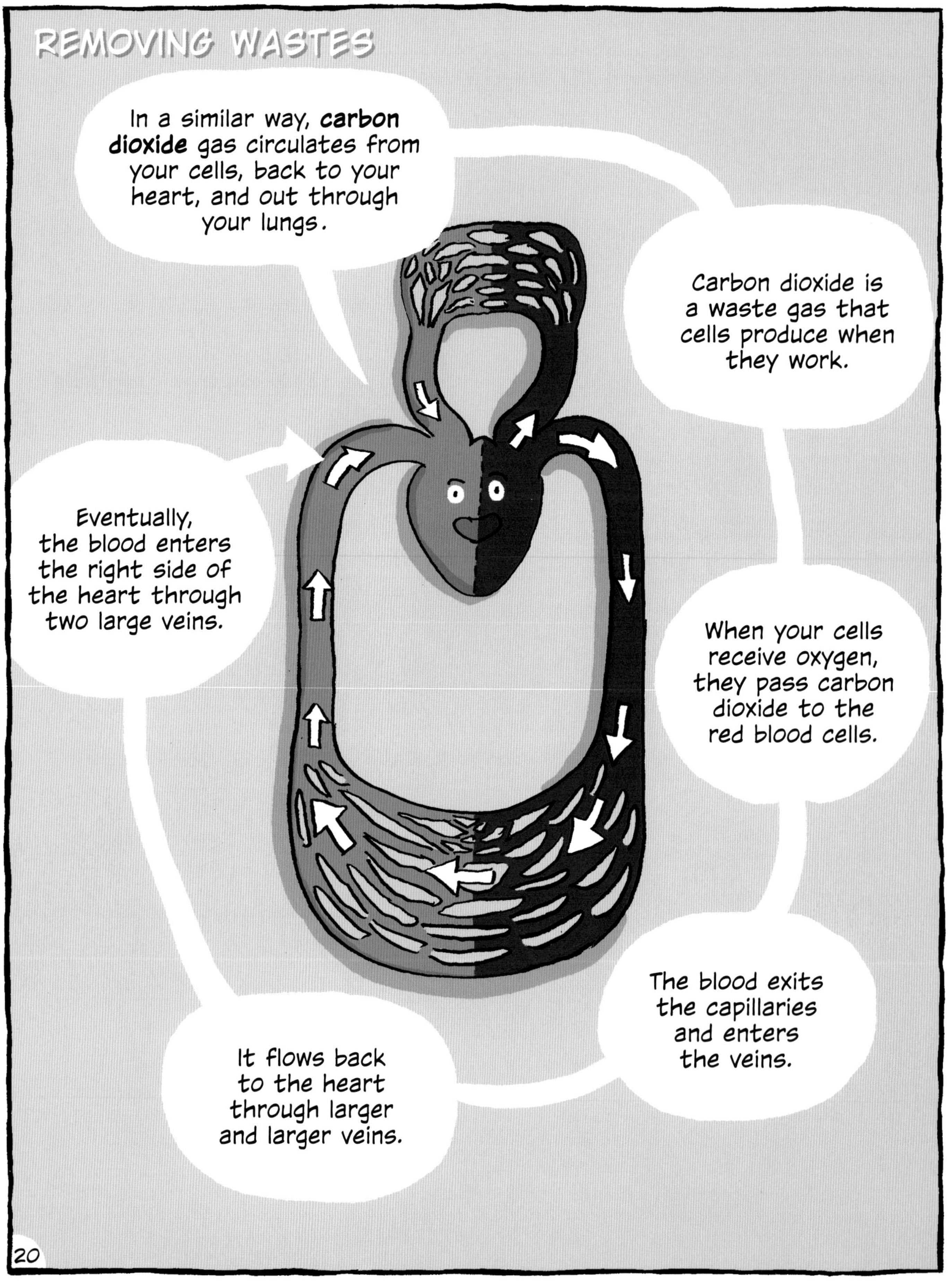
REMOVING WASTES
In a similar way, carbon dioxide gas circulates from your cells, back to your heart, and out through your lungs.
Carbon dioxide is a waste gas that cells produce when they work.
When your cells receive oxygen, they pass carbon dioxide to the red blood cells.
The blood exits the capillaries and enters the veins.
It flows back to the heart through larger and larger veins.
Eventually, the blood enters the right side of the heart through two large veins.

From the right side of the heart, arteries carry the carbon-dioxide-rich blood to capillaries in the lungs.

Carbon dioxide passes through the capillary walls into the lungs.

It leaves the body when you exhale.

When you inhale again, oxygen passes from the lungs to red blood cells in a similar way.

This oxygen-rich blood returns to the left side of the heart...

...and begins the journey all over again!

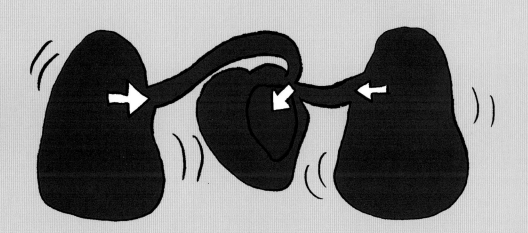

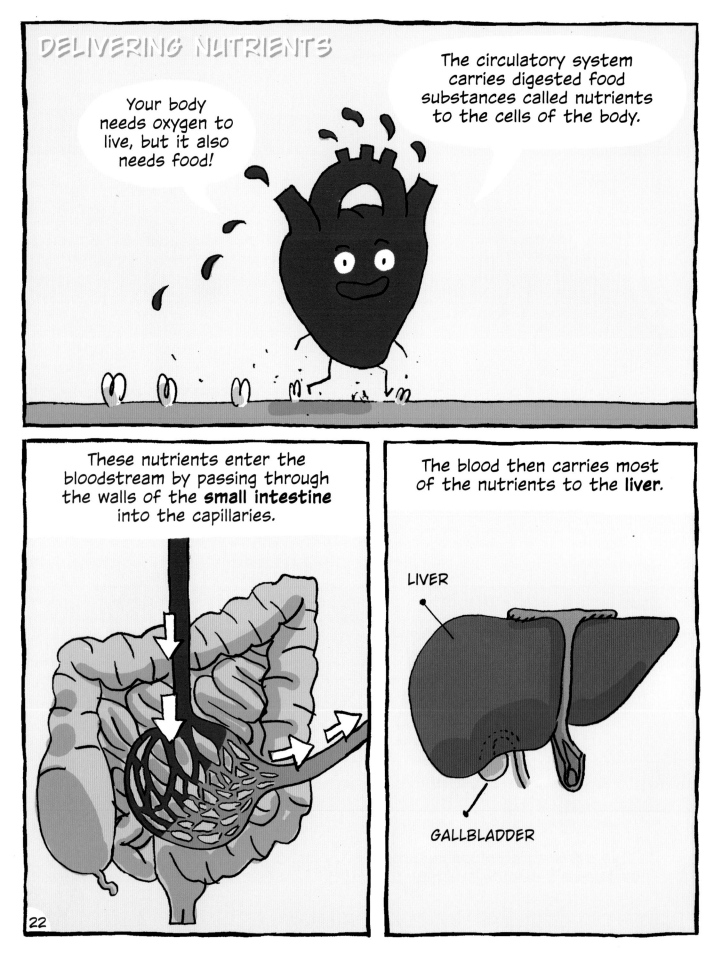

Doctors have many ways to measure the health of your circulatory system. One way is to check your blood pressure.

Blood pressure is the force of blood moving through the body.

Just as a bicycle pump forces air through an inner tube, your heart forces blood through blood vessels.

When your heart contracts, it pushes blood into blood vessels.

Arteries have stretchy walls that bulge when the high pressure rush of blood comes from the heart.

ZOOM

RING RING

Then, as the heart muscles relax, the blood slows down again and the pressure falls.

The artery walls also relax.

Just as too much air pressure in your bike tire can cause a blowout...

...high blood pressure can damage your arteries.

High blood pressure is called **hypertension**.

HOP

POP

POP

Eating a balanced diet helps to keep your heart healthy.

Vegetables, whole grains, and lean sources of protein are all good for your circulatory system!

Exercise helps your arteries stay stretchy. It also helps to keep your heart muscle strong.

This makes the heart more efficient at pumping.

Hop

Zip

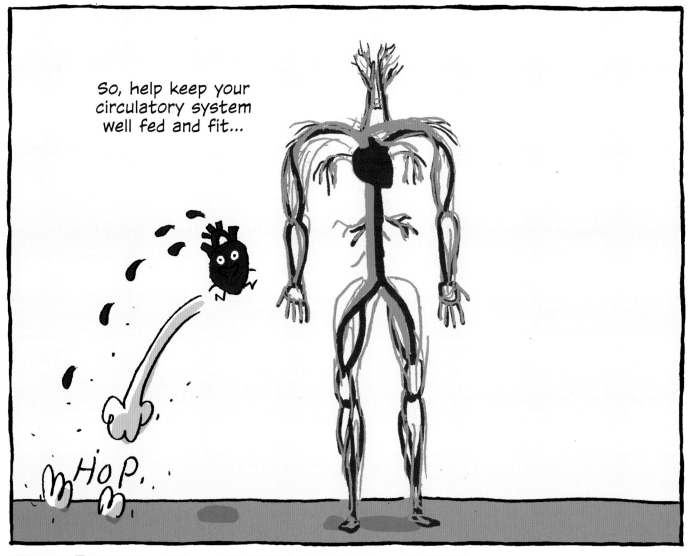

So, help keep your circulatory system well fed and fit...

HOP.

...and remember, no matter what you are doing, your heart is doing it, too!

GLOSSARY

aorta the main artery of the body.

artery a blood vessel that carries blood from the heart to the body.

atrium one of the two top chambers of the heart.

bacterium; bacteria a tiny single-celled organism; the plural of bacterium.

blood pressure the force of blood moving through the body.

blood vessel a hollow tube that carries blood and nutrients through the body.

capillary a blood vessel with a very narrow opening.

carbon dioxide waste gas that cells produce as they work.

cell the basic unit of all living things.

chamber one of the hollow spaces in the heart.

circulatory system the group of organs that carries blood through the body.

hypertension a disease caused by high blood pressure.

liver an organ in the body that functions as a chemical factory and stores energy.

nutrient a food substance that helps body growth.

organ two or more tissues that work together to do a certain job.

oxygen an essential gas that is breathed into the lungs.

plasma a clear liquid that is part of blood.

platelet a cell that stops bleeding by sticking together with other platelets to form a clot.

red blood cell a cell that carries oxygen from the lungs to the body tissues.

small intestine an organ that breaks down and absorbs food.

tissue a group of similar cells that do a certain job.

vein a blood vessel that carries blood to the heart from the body.

ventricle one of the two bottom chambers of the heart.

virus a tiny substance that causes certain infections.

white blood cell a cell that helps protect the body from diseases.

FIND OUT MORE

Books

The Circulatory Story
by Mary K. Corcoran
(Charlesbridge Publishing, 2010)

The Heart: Our Circulatory System
by Seymour Simon
(HarperCollins, 2006)

A Drop of Blood
by Paul Showers
(HarperCollins, 2004)

Human Body
by Richard Walker
(DK Children, 2009)

Human Body Factory: The Nuts and Bolts of Your Insides
by Dan Green
(Kingfisher, 2012)

The Way We Work
by David Macaulay
(Houghton Mifflin/Walter Lorraine Books, 2008)

Websites

Discovery Kids: Your Cardiovascular System
http://kids.discovery.com/tell-me/science/body-systems/your-cardiovascular-system
Get an in-depth education on all of the parts that make up the cardio-vascular system, fun facts included!

E-Learning for Kids: Heart and Circulation
http://www.e-learningforkids.org/Courses/Liquid_Animation/Body_Parts/Heart_and_Circulation/
Take a peek inside your circulatory system in this clickable lesson with bonus comprehension exercises.

FunSchool: The Heart Facts
http://funschool.kaboose.com/formula-fusion/games/game_the_heart_facts.html
Listen to a heartbeat while testing your knowledge of the human heart.

Kids Health: How the Body Works
http://kidshealth.org/kid/htbw/
Select a body part to watch a video, play a word find, or read an article to learn more about its function in the human body.

My Body: Circulatory System Instructional Activities
http://www.henry.k12.ga.us/cur/mybody/circ_lessons.htm
Perform these hands-on activities to gain a visual perspective on the heart and its role in the circulatory system.

NeoK12: Circulatory System
http://www.neok12.com/Circulatory-System.htm
Watch videos that illustrate the flow of the circulatory system, and then take grade-specific quizzes to test your knowledge.

Science Kids: Human Body for Kids
http://www.sciencekids.co.nz/humanbody.html
Sample a range of educational games, challenging experiments, and mind-bending quizzes all while learning about human body topics.

Watch Know Learn: Circulatory System
http://www.watchknowlearn.org/Category.aspx?CategoryID=805
Over 20 educational videos present, discuss, and review the complexities of the circulatory system.

INDEX